THE LONELY
BEAST

CHRIS JUDGE

For Cliona

First published in Great Britain in 2011 by Andersen Press Ltd., 20 Vauxhall Bridge Road, London SW1V 2SA.
Text and Illustration copyright © Chris Judge, 2011. The rights of Chris Judge to be identified as the author and illustrator of this work have been asserted by him in accordance with the Copyright, Designs and Patents Act, 1988. All rights reserved. Printed and bound in Malaysia.
10   9   8   British Library Cataloguing in Publication Data available. ISBN 978 1 84939 255 6

The Beasts are very rare.
Not many people have
heard of them.

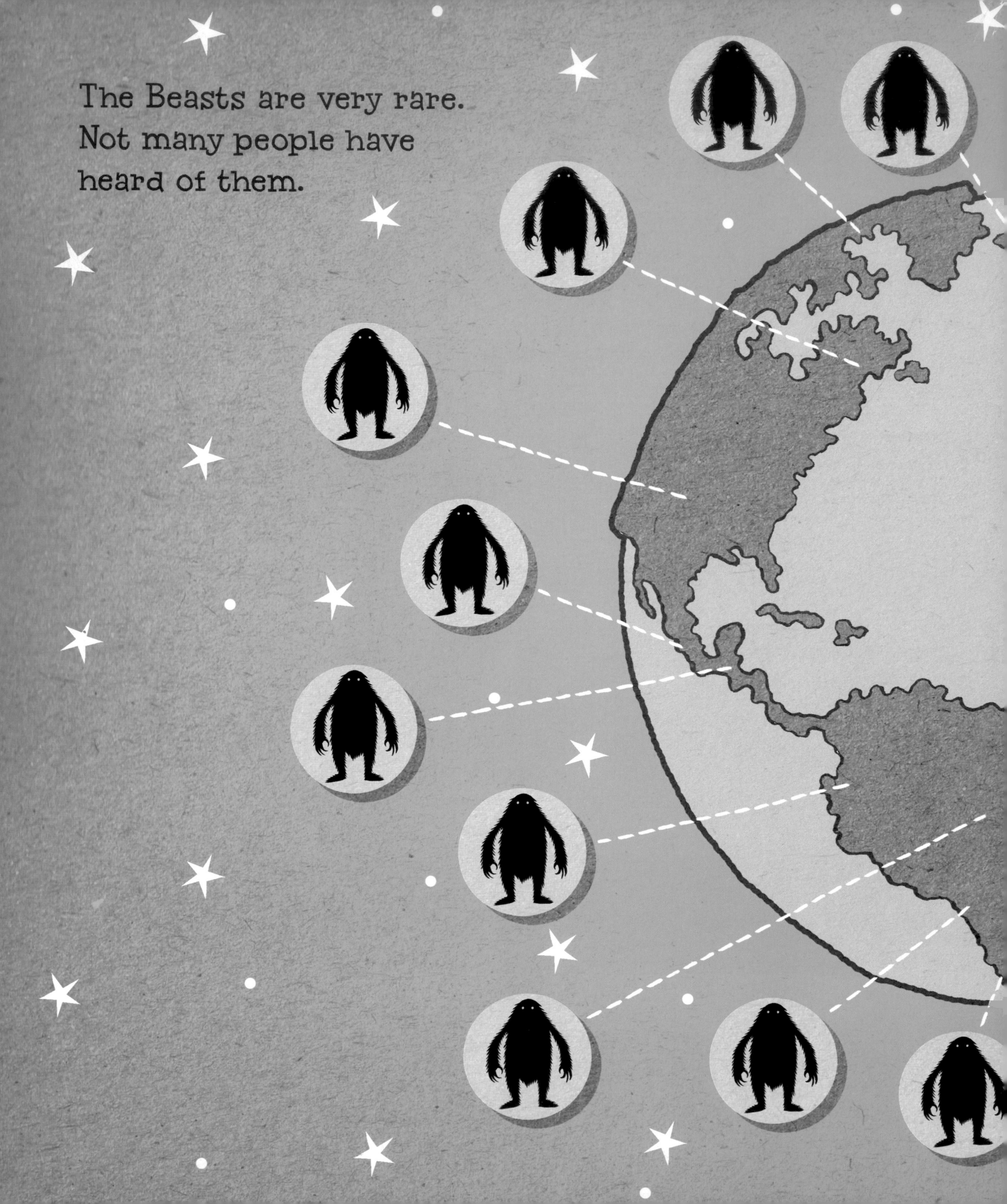

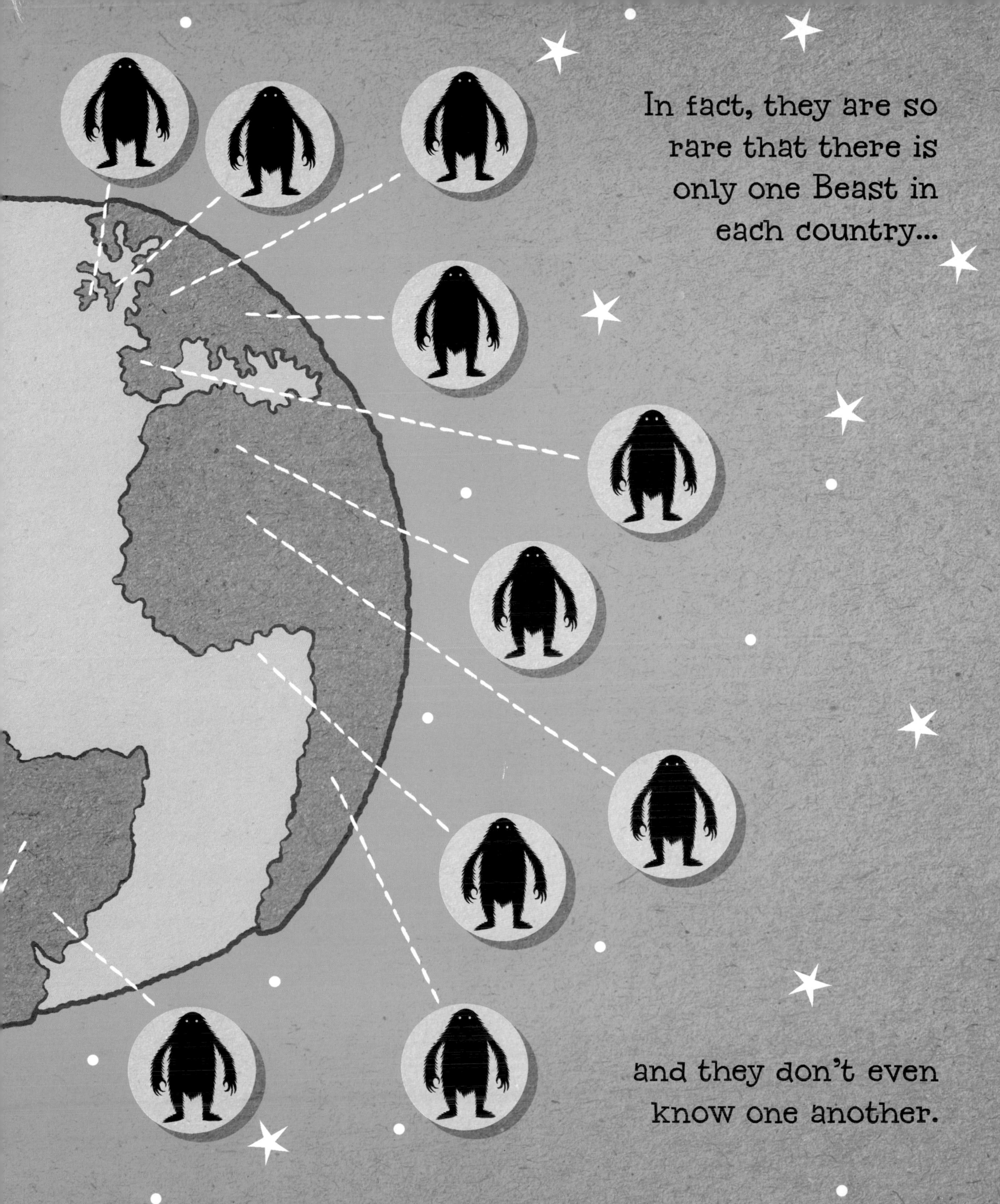

In fact, they are so rare that there is only one Beast in each country...

and they don't even know one another.

They are very quiet creatures, who live alone high
in the mountains or deep in the woods.
They like nothing more than tending their
beautiful gardens...

drinking tea...

reading a good book...

walking in the snow...

standing in the rain...

baking cakes...

and, of course, eating them.

This is the story of one such Beast who,
one day, suddenly felt very lonely.

He made up his mind there and then that he would go and find some other Beasts.

Straight away he started walking through the forest...

and stumbled down the side of the mountain.

He crossed a
dangerous river...

climbed down a
high cliff...

jumped off a giant
waterfall...

and crept through
a dark cave.

He ran over many
snowy mountains...

and finally he reached the sea.

He jumped in and
started to swim...

until he could no
longer see land.

A seagull rested on
his head...

and he played with
some dolphins.

He swam and swam and swam,

until he was very, very tired.

So he started to sink...

and when he reached the bottom, he started to walk.

On the way he was nearly caught by a huge octopus...

trapped his foot in a giant clam...

walked through a garden
of pink jellyfish...

and swam with a
giant turtle.

Just when he could swim no more, he hitched a lift from a friendly whale.

Then he walked...

and walked...

and walked...

and walked...

and walked.

Until he arrived at the city and saw lots of people, but there were no other Beasts.

"Hello," he said, but everyone ran away!

Curious, the people slowly came back to meet him...

and soon the whole city came out to say "Hello".

The people liked the Beast so
much they let him live in the big park.

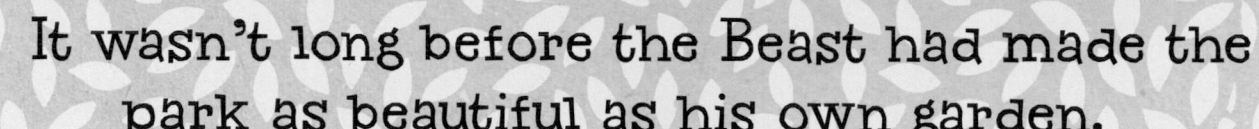

It wasn't long before the Beast had made the
park as beautiful as his own garden.

Every day people came to visit him.

He liked the people very much, but he was still lonely.

So he decided to talk on the radio...

and to all the newspapers...

and on television, about his great journey to the city and his search for other Beasts.

Suddenly the whole world was talking about him.

But still he had not heard from any other Beasts and he started to miss his own garden.

Hurrying through the streets, he left the city.

He walked...   and walked...

and walked...   until he reached the sea.

Then he started to swim until he was very, very tired

and sank to the bottom

and walked some more.

He trapped his foot

and nearly got caught

before reaching the shore.

He climbed the cliff,

crossed the river and finally found his forest.

He was amazed to see so many other Beasts in his garden!

HOME ☆

They had been
feeling lonely too, and
had come from all
over the world
to find him.

They danced through the night and every night after that. And the Beast never was lonely again...

The End